The Prototype's Descendant

A Terralien Novella #1

Maria Rosera

Paisley Press Books

The Prototype's Descendent
Paisley Press Books
Printed in the United States of America
First Printing: June 2017

ISBN-13: 978-0-692-90089-5

Edited by There for You Editing Services
Cover design by Desiree DeOrto Designs

To Rob,

You are my match in every way.

I love you.

CONTENTS

The Prototype's Descendant

CHAPTER ONE

KYLA

It was not how I envisioned the start of my road trip. Not even close. If someone else claimed it happened to them, I wouldn't have believed them. Yet as I look down at the world below me, I know I am living proof it's true. I often find myself wondering what would have happened had I not hit that stupid pothole. Although, knowing what I know now, I'm not sure I would have done anything differently. That pothole was unavoidable anyway. The only way I could have missed it was to have not been on that road at all, but in New England, potholes are everywhere. If it wasn't that one, it easily could have been another.

My boyfriend, Dan, and I were driving down a dark country road while on the first leg of a road trip. It was the start of summer break, and we were celebrating his graduation from culinary school. I still had another year of college at the state liberal arts school. High school sweethearts, our colleges were only fifteen minutes away from one another, but that didn't necessarily make things any easier, and our relationship had been suffering as a result. I could tell we were growing apart. It was one of the reasons why I suggested a road trip. We always talked better when in the car getting away from it all, as if physically putting distance between us and our problems made it easier to talk about them. Lately, we did a lot of things better in the car as we escaped from strict RAs, nosey roommates, and the

"

same old thing in search of private time together. Maybe that was part of the problem.

Truth was, I didn't know where we were going anymore, and I didn't mean on the road. I didn't know if this was the last hurrah—a way to part amicably as friends—or an attempt to save our relationship. I believed it was the former. I was no longer sure if we would continue to play romantic roles in one another's lives. After five years, we had become different people. Not in the way we had been, anyway. I was desperate to travel. There were so many things I wanted to see. Dan had little interest in going much farther than a few hours away. He didn't understand my desire to go to Paris for the fall semester of my senior year to live amidst the art and architecture I studied and loved. I didn't understand his desire to open a barbecue food truck and butcher his own meats for it ... but at least *I* was supportive.

Shortly into the trip, Dan suggested we pause our relationship to figure out what we really wanted. I couldn't say I was surprised. At least we were on the same wavelength. He asked if I wanted to go home, put an end to our road trip before we could get any farther down the road, but I wanted to keep going. I had been looking forward to this trip for weeks. And even though we were taking a break for the summer, that didn't mean we couldn't still hang out as friends.

I had a lot of time to think things over as Dan slept—the only noise to keep me company the sound of my engine and Dan's hushed breathing. He couldn't sleep with the radio on. As someone who regularly fell asleep with the TV on as background noise, I didn't understand that, either. He was one of the lightest sleepers I knew.

When I hit the pothole, my first thought was, *How in the world did he not wake up?* I swear that sudden bang as the tire dropped into the pothole would have jolted me awake instantly. I was grateful he stayed asleep, though. He was always grumpy if he didn't wake up on his own terms.

When I hopped out of my car to check the damage, my front driver's side tire was already completely flat. Opening the trunk, I grumbled at my bad luck but tried to reason with myself. There had been no way to avoid the pothole. Had it been daylight, I would have seen it sooner and could have taken it slower or swerved to not hit it straight on. It was too big to have missed it completely. At least I knew how to change a flat. I cursed at the number of things we had on top of where my spare was stored. It didn't help that the only light I had came from the trunk's interior light.

We were too far out into the country for the roads to have streetlights, and what moon there was in the night sky was hidden by clouds.

I grabbed my purple duffle bag to get it out of the way, slinging it over my shoulder, just as a spotlight appeared over me, lighting up my whole car and the road around it.

CHAPTER TWO

JEREMIAH

I had no say in who would get taken. All I knew was that *someone* was getting taken and when. But I wanted to know who, too. I didn't want to rely on reading the file on my retinal display—a *retna*—as I walked to the intake room. It didn't give me enough time. Wanting to take initiative and get more involved so I could put my best foot forward, I had asked once if I could help choose who we'd take. I had ideas on screening subjects so we would have a better shot of finding what we were after. But my superiors had yet to listen to me. According to what they told me, that was above my pay grade and those decisions were usually made on the moon base, not on the spaceplane.

I had been doing this job for three years on this ship, and I had yet to be promoted. You make one mistake with the knife during your rookie mission, and they never take you seriously or let you live it down ever again. Yet they didn't fire me; it wasn't a job enough people wanted. Stars, I didn't even want the job, but it was a necessary one on my path to the job I desired.

"Butch to intake for eval."

I rolled my eyes at the nickname as I started the trek to the outer ring of the floating spaceplane. Yeah, they called me Butch, short for Butcher. Unfortunately, after three years, I figured I was stuck with it. It wasn't completely my fault that I had sliced off the man's ear during my first night on the job. He hadn't been given enough paralytic and jerked when I started to make my incision. Fortunately for him, I scanned his ear into our bios replicator and made him a nearly exact replica using his own DNA. They didn't fire the *paralastysiologist* for his mistake, either, but we hadn't worked together since at my request. Thank the stars he wasn't the only one on board.

As I slowly walked toward the medical wing, I read through the Terralien's preliminary intake file on my retna. I liked to go into an evaluation with as much information as I could, but it was never enough. The moon base in charge of compiling these files never forwarded us more than vital statistics.

It had been a while since they had taken a Terralien remotely close to my age. This girl was twenty-one, an age when many Terraliens were close to finishing their higher education. At twenty-two, I had been out of school already for five years, and that was after staying in school for as long as I possibly could. Granted, our schooling was conducted at an accelerated rate, but that's what happens when you can literally learn something while you are sleeping. I had used night school to take electives in Terralien culture. I took a refresher course on the subject each year to stay as current as possible. The changes from year to year were astounding. I found Terraliens fascinating. Such a small microcosm in the universe, yet so unique. No two exactly the same. They were so much more than the "specimens" my job referred to them as. I hadn't seriously called a Terralien that ever.

Maybe that's why I had such problems with my job, aside from them not taking me seriously. I couldn't understand why everyone looked down on the Terraliens. Sure, we were ahead of them technologically by at least a century, but we weren't any better than them, not really. We had once been just like them, minus the obsession with what they call reality television.

The truth of the matter was we needed them.

Our survival depended on them.

Pushing open the double entry doors to the medical wing, I walked down the sterile hallway until I came to the second door on the left and turned to head straight into the intake prep room. The rest of the eval crew was already there; the two assigned to intake transportation were walking out of the exam room. They must have just wheeled her in from the acquisition chamber.

"Hey, Butch. Remember to keep this specimen intact, eh?" one of the intake crew teased as I walked to the prep room sink.

I could only roll my eyes and cringe internally at the choice of words as I disinfected my hands. He walked out of the room. Thankfully, the jokester wasn't a part of the eval team. I didn't want that type of attitude in with me when I worked. I glanced through the window of the door to the exam room and saw the same paralastysiologist I had been working with on the infamous night of the ear incident. He smiled as he saw me and winked.

Ugh. This guy was a black hole, a real jerk. I'd take the jokester on the intake crew any day. I shot a look back over my shoulders at the two members of the crew doing observations. Twins, both of them shrugged their shoulders. I doubt he was their choice, either. Pavel must have been sick—and there was no way he would be allowed near a Terralien if he was. It was too risky to expose a Terralien to our illnesses. Walking through the doorway as the cold, forced-air disinfectant removed contaminants from my hair and clothes, I had a sinking suspicion it was going to be one of those nights.

"Careful with that knife there, Butch," Jaxon warned, chuckling, as I reached for the scalpel.

"Just make sure you've given her enough paralytic. You're just as responsible for that night as I am ... if not more." I walked over to the gurney to get a closer look at the young woman I was about to evaluate. Looking down—scalpel in hand, and ready to make the first cut—I saw her face for the first time. "Oh my stars. She's gorgeous."

CHAPTER THREE

KYLA

My hearing was the first thing to come back to me. I had no idea who had said that. *Who is gorgeous? Is he talking about me?* It wasn't a voice I knew, and I couldn't place the accent. It had a lilt to it, but it was strange and unlike the kind you would expect to hear from someone from Ireland or Scotland. All I knew was it wasn't Dan, and alarm bells started going off in my head. *Where is Dan? I remember hitting the pothole and my tire going flat. Did something happen when I was changing the tire? Did I get hit by another car? Is Dan okay? Is this an EMT? Ugh. Commenting on my looks when you're supposed to be helping me, how unprofessional can you be?*

Slowly, feeling crept back into my body. I hadn't realized how numb it had just been. I hadn't felt anything at all, but now I could tell I was on something cold. Metal. *Am I in the hospital?* I had no idea where I was, but lying on a metal table was definitely not where I wanted to be no matter what. My eyelids felt heavy, and I fought to open them. In that moment, I almost wish I hadn't.

Leaning over me with a knife in hand was a guy with olive-green skin. And he was smiling—not some crazy, maniacal smile, but one that seemed nice, a smile you gave when you were completely taken with someone ... *Taken? Taken. I've been taken!* The mental fog I didn't realize I had suddenly vanished. There was a man leaning over me with a knife! This was no EMT. I bolted upright and backward, slamming into a cold gray wall. Ripping the tubes from my hands, I rolled myself off the gurney, my feet hitting the hard floor and my knees buckling. As much as I tried, I couldn't stand up. Why wouldn't my legs cooperate? There was no getting out of here if I couldn't run away, not that I knew where I was to begin with, but I highly doubted it was a hospital. Not when the guy looked like that. Was he really green? I crawled to the corner of the room and curled into a ball, covering my vital organs and my neck.

"Butch, do something, would ya?" That was not the voice I had heard before. *Oh my gosh! There are two men in the room!* I tried to make myself even smaller.

Something clattered to a metal surface. "What do you expect me to do? You messed this one up." It was the first voice, and boy, was he not happy with the other guy. "You're the paralastysiologist, and guess what? She's awake and she moved. A lot." Part of me appreciated the snark he was spewing at the other guy, but I didn't miss the fact that they were talking about me. *What the hell are they going to do to me?*

"At least you didn't cut off her ear."

Quickly, I felt each side of my head. They were both still there. I let out a small sigh of relief. I don't know why, but that made me feel a whole lot better.

"And that time was your fault, too."

The first voice was much closer this time. I could hear the other man talking but couldn't make out any of the words. *Are they even speaking English?* I peeked under my arms and spotted two green feet pointed in my direction about a foot away. People weren't green naturally, and it wasn't some sort of tattoo. Why would someone have chosen to make themselves a solid color? A ludicrous thought popped into my mind. *I've been abducted by aliens, haven't I?* But aliens weren't real, they were just something from Hollywood and those conspiracy shows on the channel that used to be about real history.

"Are you okay?"

Is he talking to me? I heard him shift slightly and then felt a hand gently touch my shoulder. I recoiled. "Don't touch me," I growled. "Get away from me!"

The hand fell from my shoulder, and I saw the feet shuffle back a few inches. "I'm not going to hurt you. Come on out."

"Says the guy who was holding a knife over me. Thanks, I think I'm good right here." Like I'd fall for that falsity. I'm not an idiot.

"It was a tiny scalpel, and if you'd look up, you'd see I put it down. I'm not going to hurt you. I promise." He let out a sigh tinged more with defeat than frustration. "Please?"

I don't know what it was about the please that made me want to listen to him. Perhaps it was how it was laced with the same defeated sound as his sigh but with an ounce of hope mixed in. I couldn't see how that sort of emotion would shine through if he was going to hurt me. Oh my gosh, was I actually starting to believe him? I mean, he easily could have overpowered me by now, and he hadn't. He even backed away when I told him to. I slowly lifted my head so that my eyes peeked up from behind my arm that was still across my face.

Staring back at me was an olive-green face with hunter-green green freckles over the bridge of its nose. The guy had dark-brown hair and stars in his eyes ... literally. I could make out constellations in his eyes.

One thing was certain, though.

"Oh my goodness ... you're human!"

CHAPTER FOUR

JEREMIAH

As scared as she was, she saw right past our differences. This hazel-eyed, auburn-haired petite supernova looked past my green skin and starry eyes and saw the truth. I *was* human. "Mostly," I answered in all honesty.

Lifting her head up all the way, she faced me head on. She remained seated with her knees pulled up and her arms across her chest, but this was progress. "What do you mean *mostly?* That seems pretty cut and dry to me. Either you are or you aren't."

That made me chuckle. She had a point. "There are a few differences down at the cellular level from our having lived off of Terral for several millennia, but we are more closely related to you than you are to chimpanzees or gorillas."

"You know what chimpanzees and gorillas are?"

"I don't know if everyone here on board the spaceplane does, but I have been studying Terral for fifteen years. I am well aware of the animal life on the planet."

"Terral?"

"You refer to it as Earth. It's not such a foreign word when you think of it. It's originally how you got the word *terra.*"

She relaxed her arms, and they fell to her sides. *Good.* If we were going to get her out of this safely, she needed to trust me. I knew we only had a couple of minutes at best before a crew would come in to deal with her. I wasn't going to let them hurt her. An idea was shaping in my mind. I could only hope my superiors would go along with it.

"So are you saying that you used to live on Earth?"

"Just how old do you think I am? I said several *millennia*. So, no, not me. But my distant ancestors did, yes."

She eyed me skeptically as she pondered my question. "Do you age like me?"

She was smart, and I liked it. "Yes, there's nothing like calculating your age in dog years or anything if that's what you're asking," I said, using a Terralien phrase I hoped she'd understand.

I knew she was still afraid—her doe-eyed stare stayed locked on my face—but she smiled then, albeit slightly. It warmed my heart, and that warmth rose to my cheeks. I wondered if she could tell the difference the blush created in my complexion, if she knew of the effect she was already having on me.

She scrunched her lips up sideways. *Adorable.* "Twenty-five."

"Close, I'm twenty-two."

"Really?" she said with surprise but as if she didn't quite believe me. "How old do you think I am?"

"Kyla, I know for a fact that you are twenty-one."

Her body went rigid, and her eyes grew even wider. *Aww, comet!* I shouldn't have said that.

"H-how do y-you know that?" she stammered, casting her eyes to the floor.

There was nothing I could do but tell her the truth. If I lied now, there was no way she'd trust me later. "Kyla, I don't mean to alarm you, but we didn't take you by accident. We've had an eye on you for some time."

She fought a shudder with a deep breath. "Well, you kind of failed with that whole not alarming me part. I wasn't supposed to wake up, was I?" I shook my head, and she grew quiet. "And how is that fair?"

Her question caught me off guard. "How is *what* fair?" There were a few things she could be referring to, and I could easily see how she would think getting taken wasn't fair. It wasn't, even with the precautions we took to return Terraliens to where they came from and to prevent them from remembering, but we didn't have a choice if we wanted to find a way to survive.

"How is it fair that you know all these things about me but I don't even know your name?"

It was my turn to smile. I couldn't say I had been expecting that. "You have a point. My name's—"

"Butcher! What are you doing? Apprehend the Terralien!" a booming voice startled me.

Aww, comet! Time's up.

Kyla threw her arms back over her head, covering her face once more.

"I promise I am not going to hurt you," I whispered to her as I bolted upright and spun around to face the commander.

"Commander, this isn't usually your duty, sir," I said, trying to sound as casual yet as in control as possible. I saluted him, his face darkening with the fury of a black hole.

He stood rigid, flanked by two of his advisors. "Well, it's not often that I have the same crew screw up so royally multiple times."

My façade cracked slightly as I tried to defend myself. "Sir! I had nothing to do with this. Jaxon is responsible for administering the paralytic. I had not even begun to conduct my examination before the Terralien woke up and fled to the corner."

"Well, it doesn't look like you were helping him to secure her."

Helping? More like he hadn't even tried to help *me*. He just stood there after pressing the alert button for help. Not that it mattered, I wasn't going to have that space cadet go anywhere near Kyla after what he did. "Sir, I had everything under control."

"Then why is she still on the floor? Jaxon, administer another round of paralytic. Then, come find me in the command center. Butch, you can continue with your exam when the paralytic takes hold." The commander turned to leave.

There was no way I could let Jaxon touch Kyla, even when given a direct order. "Sir! You can't let him do anything to her after screwing up so badly! Look at him, his nerves are shot. What if he screws up even more?" Jaxon, who had been worrying the front of his shirt between his hands, immediately stopped and stood still, but the number of wrinkles in his otherwise immaculately-pressed brown uniform gave away his state of mind.

"Are you questioning my authority, Junior Physician Taylor?"

Comet, if he's using my actual name and title—he's close to blasting off. I quickly looked back at Kyla and knew I had to push what could be my commander's next-to-last button.

"Yes, sir. I am, sir." I watched a new wave of heat rise up the commander's neck. "May I explain, sir?"

"You better make this a good one, Taylor, or you will be following Jaxon to command."

Saluting him, I made my proposal, hoping Kyla would go along with it. "With all due respect, sir, I believe that we should try a new approach with the Terralien. She's awake and responsive, so why not use that to our advantage? Why not get an in-depth look into her psyche, attitudes, and beliefs through actual conversation? Sir, this could be a one-time opportunity to learn more about the Terraliens from a real Terralien and not just a night course."

"And do you presume to be the one to undertake this assessment?"

"Yes, sir. I know you are aware of my advanced diploma in Terralien studies."

He sighed. "I am. Your mother won't let me forget it."

"*Dad*, please." That was absolutely his last button.

Directing his gaze at the ground, he pinched the bridge of his nose. Thank the stars, I knew I had him where I wanted him. "Jeremiah, do you think you can handle this responsibility?"

I bent down and faced Kyla. After burying her head into her arms upon my dad's entrance, she had peeked back above them at some point to watch the exchange, but she was still hidden from the nose down. She stared at me with questioning eyes. "Kyla, I need you to trust me. I won't let them hurt you." I gently touched her arm.

"What do you want me to do?" she mumbled.

"All I am going to do is ask you questions to find out more about you, and in return, I will answer any questions you have."

"*Any* questions?"

I glanced at the commander, my dad. He wasn't going to like my answer, but I wasn't expecting her to ask sensitive information about our operations. Who would she tell? Who would even believe her if she did? "Yes."

Lifting her head back up, she timidly asked, "Can I start now?"

"You have a question already?"

She smiled. It was almost as if she was excited by the possibility of what we would be doing. "Tons."

"Let's have it, then."

"You were interrupted before you could tell me before. What's your name?"

CHAPTER FIVE

KYLA

"Jeremiah."

I didn't know if I fully trusted Jeremiah—how could I, given how I first saw him—but I knew for a fact that I didn't want that Jaxon guy to do anything to me. He was shaking in his boots ... no way was he coming near me with any sort of drug. Hell, he wasn't coming near me, period.

Truth be told, I was curious about Jeremiah's plan. And, on some level, I was actually curious about his people, too. Who else could say that they got to ride on a spaceship and meet real aliens? Plus, their art and architecture must be fascinating. It had to be way cooler than what I had been preparing to study in France. A darker thought crept into my mind. *What good would it do me to not cooperate? It would be better to play it nice and stay safe, hoping it would mean I could avoid being drugged.* I quickly pushed the notion away. Thinking like that would do me no good. I looked up into Jeremiah's entrancing eyes. I may not have fully trusted him, but I was beginning to believe that he genuinely didn't want to hurt me.

I held out my hand. "Well, Jeremiah, are you going to help me stand?"

Jeremiah extended his hand, and I took it, glad to be getting off the floor. I was pretty sure my butt had fallen asleep, although that could have been whatever that stuff was that they did put in me. Fortunately, I had regained some control over my legs, and I took two cautious steps toward

Jeremiah as he pulled me up. His hands were slightly cool to the touch, but it didn't take long for his hand to warm in mine. This was new to me. Every boy I had ever held hands with had hands that were warmer than mine. Dan was a downright furnace, great in winter, but stifling in the summer. But Jeremiah was cool, and this sensation was different ... and, surprisingly, not unwelcome. It provided me with just enough comfort— something I was so desperately craving in that moment. *I can do this, right?*

I smoothed down the back of my shirt, thankful that whatever procedure they had planned on doing before this happened allowed me to keep my own clothes on. I tried looking on the bright side of things. It could have been a lot worse. I dropped my free hand back to my side. "There, that's better."

Jeremiah, who had kept his eyes on me the whole time, mouthed *thank you* before spinning back around to face his father. I couldn't help but feel for the guy. It couldn't be easy to have your dad be in charge and have to work for him.

Jaxon, the worried worker when he was first reprimanded, became cold as soon as I stood up. His demeanor screamed hostility. And just a few minutes before, I'd started to feel bad for the guy for being so scared. It was like he had become a totally different person now. I didn't want him coming near me with a ten-foot pole. One, not that I wanted him to do his job, but I severely doubted his competency given the situation I found myself in. Two, the daggers he was shooting at me with his glare caused the wrong kind of goosebumps to rise up along my arms. I hoped that whatever repercussions he would receive in Command Center for failing to do his job would keep him far away from me for however long I was going to be here. I didn't trust him at all.

"Sir, may I present Kyla Carver, our first Terralien exchange student."

Exchange student? Interesting ... I wasn't expecting that. Just how long did Jeremiah expect to keep me here?

CHAPTER SIX

JEREMIAH

I could have gone into hyperdrive when she agreed to my plans, at least, for now.

Albeit under odd circumstances, Kyla was the first girl I had ever introduced to my father. He had held the position of commander for the last five years, and I think that intimidated the already limited dating pool on the spaceplane.

Addressing Kyla, he said, "So I guess I should welcome you aboard the SP Perihelion. My name is Commander Taylor, and I run this spaceplane. I'm sure you'll find your stay ... interesting. Should you need anything, Jeremiah will be able to assist you." Taking a sterner tone, he added to me, "But don't think this will get you out of any of your other duties. You are expected to be here on time tomorrow. However, you may have the rest of the day off. You are dismissed."

My father spun on his heels and strode out the door, barking, "To Command Center, Paralastysiologist Jaxon Bahrber. You have five minutes."

Jaxon scurried out the door, close behind my father, but I didn't miss the glare he shot our way. I hoped his screw up would result in his finally getting fired.

The door slid shut, leaving Kyla and me alone. She took a deep breath, the tension leaving her like falling stars.

She turned to face me. "So you're really an alien, huh? You aren't just some guy in green paint? This isn't just some elaborate joke?"

I grinned. I knew she was trying to make light of her situation, but I partially did it to hide my gut reaction to the green paint comment. It was no laughing matter. Our being green was part of the reason why we needed the Terraliens. "This is no joke. Yes, to you, I am an alien, but I prefer the term Asterral." I took a step forward and then another. Grasping her hand, I gently squeezed. "Shall I show you to your room?"

She didn't answer but fell in step with me as I began walking. She was quiet for several moments, but then she finally asked, "Do you have a planet?"

"We do, although I haven't been there for several months. With only a few short breaks here and there for the crew to rest, this spaceplane has been hovering over what you call North America for years."

CHAPTER SEVEN

KYLA

"Years? Why? To take people? Why do you abduct people? Why me?" I could feel my eyes grow wide. Why on Earth would a UFO need to remain above the planet for so long?

"Remember I told you how, many generations ago, we all lived on Terral, humans and Asterrals alike?"

I nodded. "Yes."

"Even though we have a planet, we need to go back to Terral. Our numbers are declining. We're too similar to one another, we Asterrals. We lack a key component in our genetic makeup, preventing the population from thriving. Terraliens are much more diverse, and we were sent to try to harvest that component from the humans."

"Harvest?" I stopped walking and took a step back from Jeremiah, dropping his hand, a cold chill running up my spine. "You're killing people so you can survive? You were going to kill me?"

I think he paled. His complexion went from an olive green to a pea-soup green. "Kill people? You think we kill people? Oh, my stars, no." He rapidly shook his head. "I've never done more harm to anyone than accidentally cutting off someone's ear. And that was during my first night on the job. Perhaps harvest wasn't the right word. Our methods are much easier than killing people."

I took a deep breath to try to regain my composure. *Okay, they hadn't intended to kill me.* I still didn't know what they had meant to do to me, but learning I wouldn't have died up here gave me some comfort. "So if it's so easy, why take us at all, then? Why not just move to Earth?"

"You may have noticed that we don't look quite like anyone on Terral."

"True, but it's close, though."

"Kyla, we're green. That's not close enough."

I shrugged. "So move to a place where everyone is colorblind."

He let out a melodic chuckle. Warmth spread throughout me, expanding from my chest and reaching all the way to my toes. I found myself hoping it would be a noise I'd hear again. Often, if I could help it.

"Oh, Kyla, I wish that were a real possibility. It would make our lives so much easier. But I have been studying Terraliens for over half my life, and I know no such places exist. Plus, you can see color just fine. No, if you aren't there, then that is no place for me."

If he hadn't realized how he affected me when he laughed, he had to know by now. I could feel the blush rise on my cheeks. Why was I responding like this? Hadn't he just kidnapped me only a few hours before? And what did he mean by *if I wasn't there*? Why would he want me to be there?

Jeremiah cleared his throat. "So once I show you to your quarters, would you like a tour? I could introduce you to some of my friends and show you what they do."

"You aren't going to make me watch someone else get kidnapped, are you? I get that you aren't trying to harm anyone, but I don't think I could handle it, knowing that had just been me."

"I would never think of such a thing. *I* don't even like to do it."

That took me by pleasant surprise. "Then, why do you?"

"It's a step to the job I do want," he said matter-of-factly.

What job could possibly make him have to conduct tests on humans as a stepping stone to achievement? I was both curious and hesitant, what if it was worse? Then again, it couldn't be if he didn't like doing the testing in the first place. "What job is that?"

"I want to lead a team back to Terral. I want to live amongst the Terraliens. Your kind is fascinating."

I think I gasped. That wasn't what I was expecting him to say. Maybe it was the setting of our encounter, but I pictured him in a medical setting.

The whole idea of Asterrals needing to come back to Earth intrigued me. I had long wondered if aliens had taken part in some of mankind's greatest architectural achievements—the Pyramids at Giza, Mayan temples, Machu Pichu, and more. Maybe I watched too many alien shows on TV, but if the Asterrals had been involved, in even the slightest of ways, imagine how much their presence could help forward humankind today.

Jeremiah gave me a questioning look, almost like he was searching for approval.

"That's a ..." I hesitated, not knowing what to say, "great goal. How close are you to being able to do it?" How close was Earth to an alien invasion? Even if it was a peaceful one, I wasn't sure humans were ready to learn we really weren't alone in the universe.

"We have yet to find anyone with the proper genetic component to help us, but once we do, it will just be a matter of testing the compound we create with it on the teams assigned to go down. Testing could take a year, but barring any setbacks, integration would come soon after."

I wondered just what the genetic component they needed was. *Do I have it? Can I really help them get back to Earth? Do I want to?*

We stopped in front of a recessed doorway with a security panel on it. "Here's your new home. At least, for now."

Jeremiah keyed in a code and the door slid into the wall, revealing a sparse room with little more than a bed and a toilet. I was somewhat relieved to see these familiar objects in the room, but the cool metal walls and white linens made me think of a prison. "This is very cell-like. What, do you think I'm dangerous or something?"

Jeremiah chuckled. "That's because it is a cell." When he glanced at my face, whatever he saw had him hastily adding, "You aren't a prisoner, but the extra security could only be a benefit right now ... at least until everyone gets acquainted with your presence. You're our first exchange student on the Perihelion, Kyla, Terralien or otherwise, and we obviously weren't ready for you in this capacity. We don't have any spare normal living quarters available, but the Perihelion was built with the potential to host hostile lifeforms on board, so we do have a few cells."

I tried to smile but I couldn't make it reach my eyes. I felt like I was about to become some caged animal.

Likely doubting my facial response, he reiterated, "You aren't a prisoner, Kyla. It's going to be okay. It's only temporary. We'll go down to the commissary to get some supplies to make it more comfortable for you. Plus," he continued, stepping inside and pointing to the side of the door, "you can hit this button, and I'll come running."

I looked up to his celestial eyes, gazing openly into mine. "Every time?"

"Yes. As long as I'm not actively working on something in the intake bay, I'll come for you." He gently squeezed my hand.

Despite his reference to work, his pledge to rescue me from this cell made a real smile cross my face. Not even Dan would drop everything if I needed him, and here Jeremiah was, willing to do just that only hours after meeting him. Was he simply fascinated by having a human on the ship, one that he could interact with beyond testing them, or was there something else going on?

CHAPTER EIGHT

JEREMIAH

After the way she blanched at the sight of the cell, I was so glad to make her smile, even if just that little bit. I not only needed her to trust me for the job I had to do, but I wanted her to like me ... for me. She had yet to let go of my hand, and I was beginning to think I didn't want her to. It fit so nicely in mine, and I could feel its warmth all the way up to my shoulder. I glanced at her, her mouth moving as she looked back at me. Licking my lips, I wondered if hers would be just as warm as her hand.

"Jeremiah, did you hear me?"

Comet! I missed something she said. Get ahold of yourself, Jeremiah.

"Uh, no, sorry. What were you saying?"

"I asked if I could get a moment to myself. I need to use the bathroom."

"Oh, yeah, sure. I'll close the door and wait right outside. Just press the call button when you're done."

"Thanks." Kyla dropped my hand and stepped into her room. I pressed the passcode on the door, and it slid shut.

Without her in my sights, it dawned on me—there was a real, live Terralien on the spaceplane and she was up and talking, not just knocked out cold on a gurney. I hated my part in bringing her onto the Perihelion, but I was glad to have her here. I was amazed by her fearlessness and in awe of her openness. In spite of all that had happened to her, she didn't shy away from my touch. A broad grin grew across my face. It could easily have been the opposite, and not just because of our physical differences.

As I waited, the warmth that spread from holding her hand slowly receded back down my arm and hand, leaving them cold. I had never been so aware of my body temperature before, had never needed to take note of it before when everyone around me was the same. I liked the sensation of being warmer, and I wanted to feel Kyla's hand in mine again. I would have been lying had I said it was only for the warmth it brought. In just our short time together, she did something to me that I couldn't quite explain, but I liked it. I wondered if she could overlook my being green beyond just the level of friendship that we had started.

Oh my stars, what am I getting myself into?

CHAPTER NINE

KYLA

I didn't have to go to the bathroom all that badly, but the excuse gave me the opportunity to get my head on straight. What was I thinking, agreeing to stay on a spaceship with aliens? I must have been going nuts. What about my family? What about Dan? Were they just going to think that I disappeared? That didn't sit well with me, but what could I do?

Sitting on the edge of the bed, I closed my eyes and buried my face in my hands. "Just breathe," I whispered to myself. I knew I needed to talk to Jeremiah. There had to be a way to at least let Dan and my family know that I was okay, that I was safe. Contacting them was the only way I was going to be able to stay, and as crazy as it was, I wanted to despite how I got here. This was a once-in-a-lifetime opportunity, and Jeremiah seemed to want me to be here as much as I did. He really wasn't a bad guy. We would have been friends on Earth. Maybe we could be friends now.

I sighed deeply. I had to get back out there. I was already taking too long. Removing my hands from my face, I opened my eyes. My gaze fell to my hands, now back in my lap. My jaw dropped. What was wrong with my hand? I could swear it was turning green.

I knew I would have to tell Jeremiah—there was going to be no way to avoid it—but I was going to pretend I hadn't seen it yet. If I said anything now, I knew it would lead to tests. I wanted to do whatever it was I would be doing under Jeremiah's exchange program. I had no idea how long I was going to be here, so I needed to see all that I could while I was here. The medical wing was certainly not on my list of places to visit, especially not until I was sure Jaxon wasn't going to be there.

I stood up and walked to the door. Pressing the button, I waited all of seven seconds for Jeremiah to enter the code and the door to slide open.

Jeremiah greeted me with the most adorable smile. Contagious excitement oozed off him, making me momentarily forget my worries. I grabbed his hand, cool once more, and smiled up at him.

"Ready for the tour?" he asked.

"Absolutely."

We spent what felt like hours walking along the corridors of the spaceship. I was overwhelmed by its size and wondered how they had built it. It must have been constructed in space because there was no way I could see any civilization launching something this large from land, even if the amount of gravity differed. It would also explain the lack of any real decoration. My cell was sparse, but the hallways and common areas were not much better. Their dispensary, minus the lack of cooks and lunch aides because all of the food came in pill form, was a close comparison to my high school cafeteria, only with gray metal walls instead of painted cinder blocks. What minimal decoration there was came from copper scrollwork here and there and around the doors. I hadn't noticed it at first, but the copper gave the air a slight penny-like smell.

Jeremiah had a wealth of knowledge about the ship's layout and the crew on board. I could tell he had lived here for a while. He talked fast and barely let me get a word in edgewise. For some reason, I didn't think this rambley behavior was really him, and I wondered if he was nervous.

"And this, here, is one of my favorite rooms," Jeremiah announced as a door slid open, revealing a bank of thin computer screens running from one side of the room to the other from floor to ceiling. Alone in the room sat a girl, typing furiously away at a keyboard. Television footage and newspaper headlines flashed across the screens. I recognized the station logos on some of the displays.

"What is all this?" I asked in wonder as Jeremiah led me into the room.

He opened his mouth to speak, but someone else answered instead.

"This is the Monitor Room. Here, we monitor any mention of alien sightings from Terral—" The girl spun around on her chair and abruptly stopped talking upon seeing me. She wasn't much older than I was, if at all, but I couldn't be sure as I studied her hunter-green complexion, her cerulean-blue eyes twinkling. Her dropped jaw turned into a wide grin as she squealed and sprang up from her seat. Excitedly clapping her hands together in rapid succession, she bounded over to Jeremiah and me, her chocolate-brown curls bouncing around her face and shoulders.

"Jeremiah! Is she really a Terralien? I didn't believe you when you retnaed me. What took you so long? That was hours ago."

"Margot, meet Kyla Carver, and, yes, she really is a Terralien. Would I lie to you?" He grinned broadly at the girl's exuberance. "Kyla, this is Go, short for Margot—my little sister and Terralien Information Processor."

Margot's smile was catching, and I liked her immediately. Not knowing what else to do, I stuck out my hand. "It's nice to meet you, Margot."

She squealed again as she took my hand in hers. It was just as cool as her brother's had been. "Look, Jer, I'm shaking hands with a real Terralien! Oh my stars, her hand is so warm!"

Jeremiah chuckled. "It will make your whole arm warm if you hold it long enough."

"I see you haven't let go of her yet, Jer. What's that about, hmm?" she asked with a hint of teasing in her voice.

Oh, boy. I could see this getting awkward if I didn't put a stop to it. "So what do you do here, Margot? What exactly is a Terralien Information Processor?"

Margot turned, pulling me and Jeremiah toward the wall of monitors, and sat down in her chair. "Well, as I was beginning to explain when you walked in, I analyze all mentions of aliens in Terral, or Earth's, digital media. Anything transmitted electronically, I can scan—so photographs, newspapers, things posted on your internet, television shows, and more are all things I have access to."

"That's pretty cool, but why do you do it?"

"We have to be able to distinguish credible sightings and information to see if we need to run damage control to hide our presence around Terral or prepare for possible interaction with other lifeforms."

I gulped. "You mean there are other aliens out there?"

"You think there would only be one species responsible for all of this?" Margot asked, waving her arm behind her at the screens.

"No, but I'm just getting used to aliens being real in the first place."

"Oh, well, there are a whole bunch, and—"

"And we can talk about that another time," Jeremiah interrupted, giving her a pointed look.

"And we can talk about that at another time," Margot echoed, somewhat dejectedly, before adding, "Do Terraliens really believe in all of this?" She pointed at the central monitor as still images of Hollywood alien movies zoomed across the screen.

I shrugged. "Not everyone, and those are all movies, so people understand they aren't real. I'm sure some do, especially little kids who don't know better, but it's definitely not the majority."

"Then what about these? These seem much more serious." She glided down the row of monitors and pointed to another screen.

Following her to that monitor, I easily recognized the alien conspiracy television series I often fell asleep to. "This more people might believe in. It's a show that's been on for years now. Some of the episodes make good points."

"Like what?"

I began to explain what I could recall watching on those television shows that I found somewhat believable: help in constructing ancient sites and numerous depictions of spaceships in art from around the world from prehistoric times to the Renaissance.

Midway through my explanation, Margot glided down the row to a blank computer screen and began typing away.

Finished with her note taking, she spun around to face me. "You're pretty good at this stuff. If you stick around, you might just have to get a job here. You'd be a big help to me in weeding through all of this." Turning slightly, she and looked pointedly at Jeremiah. "Jer, please get her to stay. She's stellar."

"I'm working on it, Go." He squeezed my hand gently, and I felt the corners of my mouth twitch upward without conscious thought. If more aliens were like them, then maybe staying wouldn't be so bad. Jeremiah lifted his hand as if to look at a watch. Only, if he was wearing one, his sleeve was covering it, and before he could lift it up to check, he saw our clasped hands. Our clasped *green* hands.

CHAPTER TEN

JEREMIAH

Her hand was green. Did she know? There was no way—she'd be in hyperdrive if she knew. Theories on its cause began to stir in my head. I needed to get her out of here and calmly break the news to her. Then we could find out why this was happening to her. "Well, we should probably get going and let you get back to work, Go."

Kyla smiled. "It was nice to meet you, Margot. I hope to see you again."

"You are welcome back at any time." To me, she added, "Please bring her back tomorrow before you head to work."

It was a good idea. At least I would have someone to keep her occupied tomorrow and out of that cell. I knew she wouldn't be comfortable there for long. I hoped to get her into a real room soon, but we had other problems to deal with first.

I led Kyla out of the room at a rapid pace, but not fast enough for me to miss Margot whispering to herself, "A real live Terralien, how stellar." I was thrilled Go was as excited as I was about having Kyla here. We needed as many Asterrals on our side as we could get for Kyla to be able to stay. I hoped she'd want to stay—I wouldn't make her—but would she want to remain here after seeing her hand or would that be the last straw?

Kyla squeezed my hand. "Thank you for showing me that. It was pretty neat, and your sister is so nice. So where are you taking me now, Jeremiah?"

Had I not seen her hand, there was one other place I would have taken her, but that would have to wait. "It's getting late," I replied as I continued to pull her through the corridors of the spaceplane. "I should probably get you back to your room so you can sleep. You must be tired. I know I am." It was a total lie. I was wide awake. In truth, if Go was still at work, it wasn't even dinnertime. Dinnertime for us was dawn for Kyla. Takings were easier at night when the Terraliens were alone sleeping. Minus her time physically being taken, Kyla had been up for nearly a full day.

I knew there would be no sleep for me tonight when the time came, especially after seeing her hand. If it meant what I thought it did, it could change everything.

"Oh, okay." She seemed disappointed. I wondered if she could sense my tension. Slowing down a fraction, I turned to give her a smile.

Unable to stand to see that look on her face, I caved. "Come on, I'll take you the long way around."

We still needed to get her some things from the commissary anyway. Margot hadn't seen her hand; so as long as I kept holding it, I figured no one else would be able to see it either.

Much sooner than I wanted, but with supplies in hand, we were back in front of Kyla's room. I still hadn't fully figured out what to say to her. We stepped through her door, and releasing her hand, I pressed the button to close the door and give us some privacy.

Dropping her new things onto her bed, she turned to face me. "Jeremiah, did you just lock us in here? How are we going to get out?"

"I have my ways." I gave her a slight smirk, hoping to ease her growing anxiety. She raised her eyebrow. "The button is also a genetic scanner. It's programmed to let me out."

She gave me a tight smile. "Jeremiah," she began hesitantly, "is everything okay?"

Comet, I knew she picked up on my change in demeanor earlier. I took a deep breath. "Kyla, I don't mean to worry you, but look at your hands."

Her gaze fell, but she didn't lift her hands to look at them. "Oh, you saw that."

"You knew?" I had no idea. There was no change in her attitude. How had she been able to keep it from me?

"I saw it when I came in here by myself. I was going to tell you, but I didn't want to go back to being an experiment. I wanted to hang out with you and see the ship."

My heart sank. "Oh, Kyla, I hope you know you are already so much more than an experiment to me. As Go put it, you're stellar. But this"—I waved at her green hand—"changes things."

Her eyes widened. I was scaring her. It was the last thing I wanted to do. "Oh, comet, I'm saying this all wrong. Kyla, without having to test you, I believe you're what we've been searching for. I think you're a prototype's descendant."

"I am? How do you know?"

"Your hand is turning green through contact with me."

"So that makes me a prototype? Why? What is a prototype?"

I sat on the edge of her bed, and she sat next to me, slipping her hand back into mine. I think she needed the comfort, and I didn't mind one bit. It fit perfectly. Taking a deep breath—she was in for quite the explanation— I went on to tell the history of our interaction with life on Terral, explaining that we had genetically manipulated subsets of the population throughout the course of primate evolution. We had caused the evolutionary shift toward modern humans, creating Neanderthals, dwarves, elves, modern Terraliens, and more, including another sub-species of human that so closely resembled Terraliens they were virtually indistinguishable. They could even mate successfully with Terraliens. It was this sub-species, the one fused with the most Asterral DNA, that we needed to find to survive. These were the prototypes, the pinnacle of creation between Terraliens and Asterrals. Thousands of years after their initial creation, we weren't sure of the number of prototype descendants. We only knew they were rare. To have finally found one after years of searching was like the passing of a comet that only comes around once in a lifetime.

"So what happens now?" she asked, the worry back in her voice.

"Well, nothing tonight. Get some rest and we'll reassess in the morning."

"And in the morning?"

"We'll see."

"But—"

"Kyla, I'm not going to let them hurt you."

"Because I'm a prototype's descendant?"

I lifted my hand to her cheek, tracing her cheekbone with my thumb, it's olive color a stark contrast to her ivory skin. I scooched closer on the bed, leaning my head toward her ever so slightly. "No," I whispered on a sigh, closing my eyes as I drew her in for a kiss.

Her lips were like fire as I feathered my lips over hers, getting my question confirmed as to their temperature. They were just as warm as her hand if not warmer. At first, she remained motionless, but finally, I felt her melting into the kiss. Her lips began to move against mine, but suddenly, they were gone, and she was up and off the bed.

Standing five feet away, she apologized quickly but quietly, "I'm sorry. I can't do this. I think you should go, Jeremiah."

I rocketed to my feet. "I am so sorry, Kyla, I didn't mean— I didn't expect— I'm sorry." I took a step toward her, and she took one step back. I had to leave. She had asked me to leave. "I'm sorry," I repeated as I held my hand against the call button, allowing the system to read my genetic signature. The door opened, and I left, ashamed of myself for taking advantage of the situation.

What did I do? I am so stupid.

CHAPTER ELEVEN

KYLA

After Jeremiah left, my hands flew to my mouth, where I could still feel the sensation of his lips on mine. They had been like ice as he cautiously placed them against mine, waiting for me to react. I don't know if he felt me give in and respond just a little before I came to my senses and stood up. He didn't appear hurt when I did—he seemed almost understanding as he apologized—but I don't think he understood, not really. It had nothing to do with my being human. I knew I could overlook the fact that Jeremiah wasn't from Earth—he was plenty human. No, it was because of Dan. Even though we'd agreed to take a break, I needed to talk to him about where we stood before I could move forward.

Conflicting emotions raged through me as I lay down in bed that night because, despite my reservations, I wanted Jeremiah to kiss me again.

The next morning, Jeremiah greeted me with my duffle bag in hand. I was relieved to see that little piece of home and have some of my things. Without my brush, I had had to braid my hair to hide the fact that I only finger-combed it. Thank goodness I always kept a hair tie in my pocket.

Jeremiah didn't address the kiss. On our walk to Margot's office that morning after realizing he wasn't going to mention it, I knew I had to at least get him talking before we slipped into a deeper level of uncomfortable awkwardness. The silence of the first few minutes was killing me. In his effort to avoid mentioning the kiss, Jeremiah also had not brought up my lack of a green arm. Somehow, overnight, it had returned to its normal color. Was I not a prototype's descendant after all? Or was I one because I did go back to normal? I had a ton of questions on my mind, and right now, he was the only one with answers.

"Asterrals don't have two hearts or anything, do you?"

"Two hearts? What would make you wonder that?" he asked, raising an eyebrow at me.

"It's from one of the TV shows I watch," I explained. "The main character looks exactly like a human on the outside, but inside, he has two hearts."

"No, not us. There are aliens out there with two hearts, though, but they look nothing like Asterrals or Terraliens. Why do you ask?"

"Well, I just wondered if Asterrals were different from humans in any other ways than being green." I grew quiet for a moment as we walked, but I wasn't done. Jeremiah patiently waited as I formed the next question. "You said I'm a prototype or a prototype's descendant or whatever. Does that make me different from other humans?"

Halting mid-stride, Jeremiah placed his hands on my shoulders. I let out a sigh I didn't know I had been holding. His touch, even through clothing, sent a wave of reassuring energy through me, but goosebumps rose on my skin in response for an entirely different reason. Could he tell he had this effect on me?

"Kyla, I promise you, little about you is different from any other Terralien. Had you never found out about being a prototype's descendent, you would have lived a very normal Terralien life."

I nodded, feeling somewhat better with this knowledge. *I could be human if I wanted to be, but did I want to be?* He gave my shoulders a slight squeeze then dropped his arms back to his sides, and I immediately wanted to feel his calming grip once more. At least his grabbing my shoulders proved he wasn't afraid to touch me entirely.

We began walking again, but I had one more question on my mind.

"Why are you green, anyway?"

He coughed as if he had just choked on his spit. He definitely hadn't expected me to ask that. How could he not have—who *wouldn't* want to know? Especially given the situation. Clearing his throat, he answered, "It's the copper in the soil and water on my planet. It's sealed in a gray casing, so you might not have realized, but all of the walls on the ship are copper, too, not just the scrolled bits."

"So my color changing ability is like how my fingers turn green when I wear cheap jewelry?"

His melodic chuckle tickled my insides and stirred up butterflies that hadn't flown since early on in my and Dan's relationship. "Did you just compare holding my hand to wearing inexpensive jewelry?"

I could feel myself blushing. "Maybe? But I like holding your hand a lot more, and I don't mind the green. It's one of my favorite colors."

He pinched the bridge of his nose just like his father had the night before. This couldn't have been good. Was he going to send me in for more testing? "Kyla, it's probably best if you don't draw attention to your hand outside of your room. The corridor may be empty now, but you never know who might walk out of a door at any time."

"You didn't even notice, did you?" I waved my hand in his face. "See? All better. Just like when I take the cheap jewelry off, the green faded after a while."

Jeremiah stopped dead in his tracks and grabbed my hand, turning it palm side up and back several times. "What? How?"

"My only guess is just what I told you. The green eventually goes away."

He let out a relieved sigh. "Well, that is one less thing to worry about." He dropped my hand, and it fell back to my side with a dull smack.

Now that he knew I was all right, I thought he would be fine with some contact, but as I reached for his hand, he slipped it into his pocket. "Jeremiah, it's going to be okay. I'm not turning green anymore. You can hold my hand."

"It's not safe, Kyla. Now that you're back to normal, I don't want your hand to change again. What if it was permanent next time?"

I knew I could wear cheap jewelry for days and still have my skin turn back to normal after some time. I wasn't worried. "You— We'll figure it all out."

"Even so, I don't want anyone else to find out about what happens to you. I think it best if we just keep our hands to ourselves."

I was disappointed, but I couldn't help but smile just a little. "What are we, seven playing 'I'm not touching you' in the backseat of mom's car?"

"I'm not sure I understand your reference. Is this a Terralien game? It hasn't come up in my studies."

We continued walking as I explained what I meant by my comment, him absorbing every word like a sponge. He thought it was funny and commented that his dad had threatened on numerous occasions to turn their family spaceplane around if he and Margot couldn't behave in the passenger compartment. I laughed at how familiar it sounded to my family road trips. Beyond the color of our skin, Jeremiah was continuing to prove that the Asterrals weren't all that different from humans ... or was it the other way around?

CHAPTER TWELVE

JEREMIAH

Oh my stars, this girl was endearing, and she had actually wanted to hold my hand. I felt like, at any moment, I would float away as if the gravity on the spaceplane had been turned off. She made me feel happy, light. I had probably screwed up royally by refusing to hold her hand. I wanted to, I really did, but she wasn't green anymore, and staying that way was the best thing for her. I wanted to keep her color change a secret until I knew for sure if she was a prototype's descendant. I had little doubt she was.

The procedure was simple—when everything went according to plan—so despite the trouble we had had when Kyla was first taken, I had no fear of testing her now, but I was willing to risk waiting. It needed to be her choice, and I wanted her to get to know me. I hoped I could convince her to stay or to help us so that I could go to Terral and see her again.

After a long day at work, I stopped by Go's office to take her and Kyla to dinner. Dinner never took long, not in the dispensary anyway. That's what happened when food came in a pill form. It was the easiest way to store the nourishment everyone on the Perihelion needed for the long stretches of time that the spaceplane hovered over Terral. Dinner was mostly about socializing.

I led Kyla and Go through the dispensary line, taking the time to show Kyla how to use the machine. It was the first time she was actually eating in here—breakfast and lunch were distributed to our living quarters each morning. She seemed intrigued by the technology but was overall unimpressed with the meal.

"I would have thought it would be more interesting. You know, put a drop of water on it and watch as the pill expands to a fully-cooked meal on your plate."

I raised my eyebrow at her. What an imagination this girl had.

She shrugged. "What? I saw it in a movie once."

"I think I remember that one," Margot replied.

I had no idea if she did or if she was just supporting her new friend, but if she had seen it, Go would certainly remember it. She never forgot a thing. Literally. It's what made her so good at her job.

"This is just so boring," Kyla continued as she poured water into a glass. "No chewing, no flavor? Nothing." She popped the pill into her mouth and drank the entire cup of water while following me to a table in the back corner of the dispensary.

I sat down and took my pill, chasing it with the water. Kyla had a point. I never liked the pills. They only had the slightest flavor based on what mealtime it was. Dinner pills had a hint of an irony flavor from the protein contained inside. Meals with my family were much better, those were, at least, only dehydrated—much closer to what Kyla had described. Suddenly, I knew where we needed to eat dinner sometime soon. I had no doubt Margot and my mom would love the idea, and hopefully, it wouldn't be too hard to convince my father either.

It was then I realized it was a little too quiet in the usually social dispensary.

Everyone was staring at us. No doubt, word about Kyla's presence had spread over the course of the last day and a half. Several people had been in the exam room when I declared Kyla an exchange student, and we hadn't really been keeping her a secret. Nothing stayed a secret on the spaceplane for long.

It was the moment of truth. How would people react?

Kyla must have realized the room had fallen silent at the same time I did. She looked up at me with wide eyes. "What do I do?"

CHAPTER THIRTEEN

KYLA

Everyone was staring at me with curious but blank faces. It was a complete new-kid moment—something I had never been before, having lived in the same house for my entire life. I was not a fan of the attention, and I turned to Jeremiah, hoping he would know how to handle the situation. And what did he tell me?

"Say hello. They all know English," he murmured. "It's a benefit of being stationed over one region of Terral for so long. We've all studied it."

That didn't make me feel any better. Jeremiah dropped his hand underneath the table, and I felt a short but deliberate squeeze on my thigh. He gave me a slight smile, and the butterflies once again tickled my insides.

Okay. Maybe I can do this.

"Hi everyone," I said meekly. Clearing my throat, I tried again. "Hi. My name's Kyla. I'm from Earth, or I guess, Terral." I felt like a complete doofus.

"So our food's too boring, is it? Not good enough for you, huh, Terralien?" one jade-colored male shot my way from a couple tables over.

My stomach plummeted, and I was suddenly glad that my meal had been in pill form. "Oh, um, well, it's just, um ... tiny?"

A few of the Asterrals chuckled, and the guy who asked the question broke out into a big grin as the girl sitting next to him gave him a small shove.

"Oh, don't let him fool you, he means nothing by it. He doesn't do Terralien sarcasm all that well. He doesn't much like the pills, either. We only eat like this when on the Perihelion, you know."

"I didn't, no. So what's a normal meal like for you, then?"

I felt the atmosphere of the room start to change for the better as we discussed our food preferences. Asterrals resumed what I felt was their normal behavior; they joked and laughed amongst themselves, and whenever someone caught my eye, they smiled. It mirrored my previous cafeteria experiences, affirming everything I was coming to believe about the Asterrals. They were as human as I was. If they weren't green, I'd never notice them as being anything other than human. The flowing metallic clothes they wore might have made me think they were a little eccentric, however, or maybe bound for the runway in their futuristic garb. It wasn't really my taste, and it made me happy to have been taken while I was holding my duffle bag. Thank goodness Jeremiah had returned it to me. I still had a clean pair of jeans with me and a few more shirts. I had no idea how or if they washed clothes up here, so I needed to make mine last.

CHAPTER FOURTEEN

JEREMIAH

Had it been nearly anyone else in the dispensary opening up a dialogue that way with Kyla, I would have been thoroughly worried, but Chaz was a genuinely decent guy who liked everybody. I had already tapped him for my reintegration team once we could finally go back to Terral. His behavior was as much a test for him as it was Kyla, even though he didn't know it. He really did need to work on his Terralien social skills.

Leaving the dispensary, Margot, Kyla, and I turned down the hall toward Kyla's room. That was the next thing I had on my list: getting her out of that cell. Lost in thought, I almost jumped when Margot squealed.

"What's going on?" I asked.

"Weren't you paying attention? We're going to watch one of the Terraliens' alien shows with Kyla tomorrow! She's going to give commentary!"

I couldn't help the twinge of jealousy that coursed through me. I had hoped to have Kyla to myself this evening, wanting to show her something we had missed on her initial tour. I was excited by the idea, however. Watching the program with her would be a great opportunity to gain unique insight into Terralien culture. In truth, I was also happy that Margot and Kyla were getting along so well. Hopefully, it would be one more reason she would want to stay. Having difficulty wrangling my conflicting emotions, I asked as straightforward as I could, "Which one?"

"The one with the physician who changes faces! It's one of Kyla's favorites!"

Kyla burst out laughing, and the sound pushed out all of the lingering jealousy, igniting my insides in a completely different way. She sounded genuinely happy to be here in that moment, and I couldn't be upset with that. She needed more than just me, and she couldn't pick a better friend than Margot.

"Is that not what it's about?" Margot asked, confused. "I've only ever seen flashes of it on my monitors, and it's always muted."

Giggling, Kyla answered. "Not quite, but that's okay. I'll explain it if you need me to."

Margot grabbed Kyla's hand and started to run down the hall. Kyla seemed to think nothing of it, but I gasped. *Her hand! What's she doing?* With Go holding it, there was no way she wouldn't notice if it turned green.

The two immediately stopped in their tracks and spun around.

"What's wrong, Jer?" Margot asked, sticking her free hand on her hip.

I caught Kyla's gaze and quickly shot a look to her hand, as I replied, "Oh, nothing, sorry. I forgot to pick something up in my room. You go on ahead. I'll meet you guys there."

Great, now I needed to think of something to grab, but it was the quickest excuse I could think of. Kyla gave me a small shrug in response to acknowledge my fears of her holding hands with my sister, but she didn't let go of Go's hand. I spun around and gave the two of them a quick wave before I ended up launching Kyla's secret into the atmosphere by telling her to stop what she was doing. Didn't she care about her safety at all?

CHAPTER FIFTEEN

KYLA

"That was certainly strange of him," I wondered out loud.

"Oh, no, that's just my brother being his usual space-cadet self. You'll get used to it after a while," Margot replied, completely unworried about her brother's behavior. "Come on, let's get a jumpstart on finding the episode you want to start with, so we don't have to worry about finding it tomorrow. We'll need to hurry out of dinner tomorrow so we don't miss out on using the *hologravision*. You're going to love it."

I wasn't so sure if Margot was right about her brother. The look Jeremiah gave me—at my hand holding Margot's—right before turning away told me that there was something more to it than his being spacey. I didn't hesitate to hold Margot's hand, and it was nice that she so readily took it. Granted, she didn't know what could happen, but would she care? If I was safe with Jeremiah knowing my secret, why couldn't Margot know it, too? She was just as excited to have me here as he was. She wasn't going to do anything if I turned green. I just knew it. She was my friend.

There was one thing wrong with her hand, though. It wasn't his.

The next night, we rushed through dinner so Margot could set up the display system before anyone else could claim it. The hologravision wasn't anything like her monitor wall. For one, this display lay flat on the table in front of us.

"How exactly does this work? Standing and looking down on the screen is going to get uncomfortable after a while."

"No standing needed." Jeremiah plopped down onto the sofa and patted the cushion next to him. "Trust me, you'll get the best view from here."

I eyed him skeptically. "But I've seen it already. Plenty of times. Shouldn't you two get the best seat?" Part of me didn't want to give him the satisfaction of sitting next to him, but the other part wanted to be close.

"You haven't seen anything like this," Margot explained, pressing one final button on the display module before sitting down on the second couch.

In front of me, what I can only call a holographic projection appeared. The Eleventh Doctor and his companion beamed up from the display in 3D. The scenery was all in 3D, too. My mouth dropped, and I jumped to my feet. Running to the side of the display, I was amazed by the technology's ability to render the 2D image I had seen multiple times into 3D, filling in all of the missing information, allowing you to see all the way around the scene. I walked behind the display, discovering that I could peer through the window the actors were walking in front of and see the scene from the opposite view of the intended shot just like I would have had I been inside a real shop looking through a real window at the action taking place outside.

"This is amazing! How does it do this? If they weren't smaller than life size, I'd swear they were real!"

"We can make them bigger if you like," Margot chirped, delighted by my response. Her hand reached out to a dial on the display's podium, and the hologram increased in size. I backed up, reacting to the wall growing and quickly approaching me.

Jeremiah chuckled as I ducked, the bottom of the wall skimming my head. "It's not going to hurt you, Kyla. You can stand up."

I stood up, my body bisected by the holographic floor. "Sorry," I said sheepishly. "I'm not used to walls moving toward me. Usually, it's the other way around." I waved my hand through the scene, disrupting the imagery, which had changed scenes and now depicted the inside of the Doctor's TARDIS. "This really is so cool."

"Well, if you're cold, come sit. It's much warmer over here," Margot giggled.

"I don't think she meant it like that, Go," Jeremiah offered as I moved out of the holographic projection and approached them on the couches.

"I'm not sure that it is any warmer over here, Margot," I said, giving her a smile and sitting down next to Jeremiah. "You two run much colder than I'm used to."

"About seven degrees or so," Margot offered, completely nonplussed about her brother correcting her. I absolutely believed she knew exactly what I meant by my use of cool. Seemingly reading my mind, she added, "I know what cool means, Jeremiah. I was trying to be funny." She tossed a pillow at him, which he caught and put on his lap.

I couldn't help but smile at their antics. Two of my closest friends back home were twins who acted exactly like this, and for a moment, home didn't seem all that far away.

We watched two episodes of the show with commentary from mostly me, prompted by questions from both Margot and Jeremiah. As the credits rolled, the holographic text making me dizzy, Margot asked, "Now, what I would like to know, is when does he change faces and why?"

I turned to her, glad to no longer be looking at the display. "We have about sixty episodes to go until he regenerates and gets a new face, Margot. It will be a while before we get to it."

She squinshed her lips to the side and raised an eyebrow. "So he can't just do it at will?"

"No."

"Oh." She definitely seemed disappointed.

"Why? Do you know of aliens that can change their face at will?"

"Absolutely," Jeremiah interjected. "One of our closest allies can."

Margot squealed in delight and clapped her hands. I had begun to realize that it was how she expressed any sort of excitement. It was infectious. I had no idea what she was going to say next, but I was already looking forward to it with a big smile on my face. "Oh, yes. They can do the best impersonations. Do you remember that one summit meeting we went to as children, Jer, and we met Benny?"

"How could I forget? It was hysterical seeing a child running around wearing Dad's face," Jeremiah laughed, sending warm jitters all the way to my toes.

"We really must visit him the next time we're in his planetary system. I wonder what he's up to. It's been a few years since we last messaged with him."

"Isn't that kind of dangerous, though? Allowing someone else to run around with your dad's face? He is rather important, at least from what I can tell. What if they transformed into someone even more powerful?"

"Well, that's one positive to us being allies. It's not something we have to worry about."

I stared at Jeremiah. How could he not see that ability as potentially problematic? "You don't? But—"

"We don't because that's not our sector," Margot explained. "We focus solely on Terralien research. Our father and older brother, on the other hand, if you want to talk safety or military strategy, they would be the ones to go to."

"You have another brother?"

"Oh, yes. He's working his way up the ranks at the academy, learning to fly space planes. I'm sure Father was glad that one of us followed him into his sector. But neither of us"—she waved her arm between her and Jeremiah—"would have been cut out for that. Mother, on the other hand, was thrilled to have the two of us follow her into Terralien studies."

"And speaking of our parents. Kyla, how about we have dinner with them later this week? I promise the food is better." He chuckled as he continued, "You can actually chew it."

I looked between Margot and Jeremiah. They wanted me to meet their parents? I immediately felt queasy. Clearing my throat, I tried to cover my nervousness. "Really? Your parents must be busy. With your dad being the commander of the ship, and— What does your mom do?"

"She's the head of the Terralien genomic testing, not just for the ship but for the whole northern hemisphere of Terral. But, no changing the subject, Kyla. You can talk with her about that during dinner." Margot clasped her hands together and held them up to her face, shaking them slightly. "You really must come."

"Are you sure? I don't think your dad really likes me."

"He hasn't gotten to know you like we have, Kyla. He only met you that one time, and you have to admit, the circumstances were highly unusual."

I couldn't find anything else to question to try to dissuade them from this idea. I had always found meeting my friends' parents to be intimidating. And these weren't just any parents. Jeremiah and Margot's parents were important, and Jeremiah and Margot definitely weren't ordinary either.

"Thank you. I'd like that," I said shakily.

"You have nothing to be worried about. Mother is going to love you," Margot assured me.

Somehow, I didn't think she'd be the difficult one to impress.

"And your dad?"

"If Mom's happy, Dad's happy. You'll see, it will all be all right. Margot, will you confirm with our parents about dinner tomorrow night when you go back to the domicile?"

I didn't miss his use of the word confirm. Had he already been planning this? Were his parents already expecting me?

"Absolutely. I'll retna you if something changes."

Jeremiah stood and turned toward me. "May I walk with you back to your room?"

As if he didn't walk with me everywhere already. *Why is he asking me this time?*

I smiled, slightly suspicious of his motives in a hopeful way. "You may." I held out my hand for him to help me up, forgetting that he wouldn't take it. It hung awkwardly in the air before I put it down to push off the sofa, dampening my attitude. I said goodnight to Margot, promising we'd do this again, and Jeremiah and I left the room. I had a feeling this was going to be a long walk.

CHAPTER SIXTEEN

Jeremiah

I could feel Kyla's disappointment seeping out of her, and if I was right, I knew what was making her unhappy. Why didn't she understand that I wouldn't touch her because of her safety, not because I didn't want to? I would figure out a way to somehow. Hopefully soon. I wanted to do more than hold her hand. Numerous times while we watched the hologravision with Margot, I wanted to lean over and kiss her. The way she gently bit her lip as she watched the climactic parts had me missing much of what was going on in the show.

I hoped what I had to show her would make up for my inability to behave how I wanted to. It was one of my favorite spots on the spaceplane. It was a stellar spot to sit and think and just get away from it all. I had been here a lot in the last few days. If I wasn't working or with Kyla, I was here, trying to figure out a solution to my dilemma. This girl was like no other, and it wasn't because she was Terralien. No, there was something about her that twisted my insides and cracked my usually cool demeanor.

I had always been goal oriented. Finding Terraliens fascinating, I had wanted to study them since childhood, and that quickly transformed to leading a team back to Terral. Kyla didn't change that goal at all, but she did make me want to progress faster. Being able to live on Terral meant being able to be with her.

"Where are we going, Jeremiah? It's getting late, and I've been here long enough to know this isn't the direct path to my room." It was the first thing she had said to me since not taking her hand to leave after the Terralien show ended.

I gave her what I hoped would be a playful reply. "You'll see." Turning around to give her a smile, I saw she had fallen behind a few feet and walked with her arms crossed, her head down. My smile fell. The scene gutted me. I couldn't stand to see her this way. "It's only a little way farther. Just a few minutes."

We were walking in a secluded hallway on one of the upper levels of the spaceplane. There were only two doors on this wing—the one we had come through and one at the end of the hallway—and few had reason to come this way altogether. It was little more than a maintenance hallway, but it led to something beautiful. I wanted her to be happy when she saw it, so I did the only thing I thought would cheer her up. I stopped and waited for her, holding out my hand. It was the wrong move.

Dropping her arms to her sides, I thought she would take it. She didn't. She stopped walking and just stared at it.

I gently grabbed her hand with mine and began walking again. "Just around the bend over there." If I could just get her there ...

"Oh, so now you want to take my hand?"

Again, I had made the wrong move. "Isn't that what you wanted?" *What's the sports saying from where Kyla's geographic sector is? Oh, yeah. Three strikes and you're out.* My dumb comment was the third strike. I slowly started backing up, hoping she'd follow without realizing it.

"Well don't go out of your way to do anything on my account. Really, Jeremiah? *Because I wanted it?* What gave you that idea—was it my crossed arms? What about fifteen minutes ago when you wouldn't even help me get off the couch? What about when you refused to take it the other morning, claiming it wasn't safe?"

"That's not fair. You know—"

"Oh, don't talk to me about fair. It's not *fair* that I was taken from the side of a road and beamed up on board to have samples drawn without my knowledge. It's not *fair* that I woke up during the process, half-paralyzed and afraid for my life. It's not *fair* that the first person who showed me any sort of comfort can't bear to even touch me." She splayed her hand over her chest, pressing her fingers inward. "You kissed *me,* Jeremiah—"

"That was before I knew—"

"Knew what, that I'd turn green?" she snapped. "Well, guess what? Margot has had no problem grabbing my hand."

"But she doesn't know what could happen!" Now, I was getting angry, too. "Don't you care about your safety at all? You know your hand could turn green, yet you have no problem with her grabbing it. You think I don't want to do the same thing? Grab your hand and never let go? Pull you toward me and feel how having your lips against mine would be different if you want to kiss me, too?" Nostrils flaring, I let out a heavy breath. She had every reason to be angry. What right did I have to be upset with her? Running a hand down my face, I tried to compose myself. "It's all I can think about, Kyla," I said, much more calmly than before.

She looked at me, eyes wide and mouth agape. "Then, why don't you?" she asked timidly, the heat from her outburst evaporated.

I raised my shoulders in a half shrug, my palms turned out toward her. "I'm not willing to risk your safety. I don't want you to get hurt."

Not all of the fire had left her. "What makes you get to decide that for me? Don't you get it?" She took a step toward me. "*I* get to decide that, and you are worth the risk to me." Grabbing the front of my shirt, she pulled us toward one another and crushed her lips to mine.

Had I any sense, I would have pushed her away, but this is what I wanted. I wanted her, and I was powerless to stop it. I wrapped my arms around her, settling one hand in the small of her back and tangling the fingers of my other hand in the loose strands of her hair that had fallen out of her braid. Her lips and tongue were like fire in my mouth, and I could feel the heat from her inner star spreading through me as we continued to kiss one another. I was vaguely aware that we were moving backward, but I couldn't tell if she was pushing me or if I was leading. But I knew where we were going.

I knew when we had reached where I had originally wanted to take her. It's as if my senses, heightened in this moment, could feel the space had widened. But still, I did not break contact, afraid this moment would end if I did. Her hands roamed my back and through my hair as our tongues danced under the stars.

Kyla gasped, breaking our connection. "It's beautiful!" She ran over to the spherical window, pressing her hands against the glass. Millions of stars shone just beyond her grasp. "How are you not here every waking minute?"

I walked up next to her, hands behind my back. "I've been wanting to show you this. It's where I come to get away from things."

"Look at them all. That's amazing! I've never seen so many stars in my life. Thank you for showing me this." Linking her arm around mine, she rested her head against my shoulder.

I kissed her lightly on the top of her head. "Just wait. I'll take you back up here one night before dinner, and you'll get a stellar view of Terral."

CHAPTER SEVENTEEN

KYLA

I had been on the ship for a full week. We had developed a routine—Jeremiah, Margot and I. In the mornings, Jeremiah and I would walk to Margot's office, where I would help her wade through news of possible sightings. In the evenings after dinner, the three of us would watch something from Earth that I could help them interpret. They continued to be blown away by a certain time-travelling doctor, who, I had to explain, was not a medical doctor. We had already watched several episodes, and they told me that some of the aliens depicted in the show were rather accurate, including the one that looked like a "giant potato." If we weren't watching that, we were watching one of the alien conspiracy shows. Margot and Jeremiah often got a good laugh from it, but they said some episodes were spot on.

Word spread about our evenings with the hologravision, and we regularly had others joining us. Chaz, who had teasingly given me trouble my first meal in the cafeteria, never missed an episode after he found out about them.

The other thing that had become routine was Jeremiah's reluctance to touch me. Since the kiss under the stars, he hadn't touched my bare skin—to keep me safe and protect my secret—but I wanted him to. I hadn't stopped thinking about that kiss. I wanted more. At least I had gotten him to loosen up about touching me at all. After that night, I could hook my arm through his and we'd be fine. I didn't turn green that way—there were at least two layers of clothing separating us. Still, I missed holding his hand. I liked feeling his chilled hand warm in mine. The more I thought about it, the more I knew—they just fit. We just fit.

It all boiled down to the fact that I was willing to take the risk he wasn't ready for. Everyone I had met was so nice, aside from Jaxon—and he had been transferred to a different wing on another level of the spaceship, so I hadn't even come close to running into him. That section of the ship even had its own cafeteria. As Margot had explained it one day in her office, the majority of Asterrals were on the Perihelion to study Terralien life and find the prototype. Therefore, they at least accepted my presence. Most others had been raised by families who valued Terraliens, and it was why they had signed on to be a part of the support crew. The leaders believed that a universal opinion on Terraliens would lead to a more successful mission. Up until Jaxon, they hadn't had an issue. Then again, up until me, there had been little opportunity for an incident.

As Jeremiah dropped me off at Margot's office, he reminded me that he wouldn't be able to collect me at the end of the day.

"I'll take care of her, Jer. You go do what you have to do, and we'll see you after dinner." Margot said, ushering me inside as she shooed Jeremiah away.

Peering back over my shoulder, I watched him turn slowly away and start to walk down the hall. I hated seeing him go, especially today, because I knew he had to test another human who would be taken some time today. He had yet to divulge my secret. I wasn't sure if even Margot knew.

I sat down in one of the two chairs in the room, which had been brought in just for me. "So what shall we look at first, Margot?"

"I have a surprise for you," Margot replied as the door to the office slid closed.

I had no idea what she could be surprising me with. I hoped Asterrals had the same idea of what a surprise was as I did. Skeptical, I asked, "You do?"

"Yes. I pulled some strings and had the console over there reverse engineered to let you get a message home. I'm sorry it took all week. I know my parents would be worried about me if I didn't check in every couple of days."

"Oh my goodness, Margot! Thank you so much!" I gave her a big hug. My parents must have been worried sick! Then it dawned on me. "What do I tell them?"

She patted me on the back then held me at arm's length, staring me in the face. "I imagine that saying you are okay would be a good start, but I would prefer if you didn't mention us or where you were."

"I don't think they'd believe me. They'd probably think I was joking," I assured, walking over to the console.

Joining me, Margot continued, "That's all well and good, but it's not your parents I'm worried about. As I started to say the other day, we aren't the only aliens out here, and it's important we do not reveal too much information about ourselves. We need to assume that if we Asterrals are monitoring Terral and Terralien activity, then someone else likely is, too."

The way she said it sent a chill running down my spine. "Margot, do the Asterrals have enemies?"

She shrugged. "Don't Terrals have enemies within their own species? Why would we be any different? I mean, we Asterrals are a relatively peaceful race, but other species are not as kind." She looked me over, easily noticing my rigid posture and death grip on the chair in front of me. "And now I've scared you. I'm sorry. I shouldn't have said all of that. We rarely have issues, but when we do, the Asterrals have a fighting fleet that patrols the stars. My and Jeremiah's older brother is training to be one of the pilots. We're completely safe." She tapped the seat my fingers were relaxing their grip on. "Come, sit. You've got a message to write."

Exactly how did one write an email to their parents when faced with this situation? Obviously, the truth was out. They really wouldn't ever believe me, and I wasn't about to put my new friends in jeopardy. But lying? I had never lied to my parents—never had a reason to. I had had a lot of freedoms growing up because I had no filter and told my parents everything and they trusted me to do the right thing. This time, however, not only could I not tell my parents everything, I couldn't tell them anything. But I had to tell them *something*.

My fingers hovered over the keys after I typed in my parents' joint email address.

"Maybe start with telling them that you are okay?" Margot suggested. "I would say you could tell them that you've met some stellar new friends and have decided to join them for an epic adventure, but that may be a bit too much."

I could hear the smile in her voice, knowing she was joking with the last part. However, I figured the first part would be okay. I set my fingers to the keyboard and began to type.

Dear Mom and Dad,

I wanted to let you know that I am fine. I don't know what he'll end up telling you, but Dan and I got separated during our road trip. He didn't do anything to me. I don't want you thinking that, but I don't know where he and I stand right now. We broke up or decided to "pause" our relationship as he puts it. I really am okay with it. I met some people who are helping me until I can get home and are showing me that there's more out there for me. I'm not sure when I'll be back, but I'll let you know if it won't be soon. I just need some time, and when I can, I'll explain everything. Just know I'm okay. I'm safe.

I'll talk to you soon.

Love,

Kyla

"Margot? I'm done writing to my parents." Margot bent down and pressed a few keys, sending the message to my parents. I had to let her do it because I didn't understand the internet platform she was using at all. It probably wasn't the internet anyway. "Before you change the settings back, would it be all right if I send another message? I wasn't alone when I was taken, and I'm sure he must be worried about me. He probably has no idea what happened. He was sleeping when it happened."

I knew she had heard me, since brought up a new message screen, but all she said was, "He?"

"I'll explain when I finish this," I promised.

If I didn't know what to say to my parents, I definitely didn't know what to say to Dan. *What on earth does he think happened?* He wasn't one to jump to wild conclusions, but there were few non-wild conclusions to jump to. He was sleeping. I disappeared from the side of the road. What options were there?

Dan,

I don't even know where to begin other than I'm okay. I'm safe. I have no idea what you must be thinking. I'm with some friends who found me, and I'll be home soon. We can talk then.

-Ky

It wasn't until after Margot was sending the email that I realized I hadn't even typed "Love, Ky" to end my message. I knew he'd read into it, and if I was home, he'd try to make some joke about it to pretend it didn't bother him. And even though he had been the one to suggest the pause in our relationship, I knew it would bug him. But I didn't care about that. It was then I realized I had the answer to the question I had been wondering when we set off on our road trip. Did I still love Dan? The answer was no.

"Asterral to Kyla, are you there?"

"Hmm? Oh, I'm sorry, Margot. I got myself lost in thought for a sec, there."

"Were you thinking about this *he* you had to write a message to?" She placed her hands on her hips and raised an eyebrow, a slight smile on her face to let me know she wasn't mad at me for zoning out.

I nodded. "His name's Dan."

"And?" She shifted her weight to one foot.

"And he was with me when I was taken aboard—"

"You said that. But are you together?"

"Well, no, not exactly. Kind of?" I watched as Margot's face fell, mirroring the way my stomach dropped at the admission.

"Now, you've confused me. How are you *kind of* with someone? Don't you love him?"

"Well, that's the thing, Margot."

She walked over to her chair and sat down. Gliding over to me, she took my hands in hers. "Sounds complicated. Tell me all about it."

I proceeded to tell Margot all about my relationship with Dan. I told her everything, from meeting him in middle school to dating him in high school and now in college. I told her how we've changed over the years, that I thought we were moving in different directions, and how I felt him close off from me in the recent months. I confessed that we had broken up and I didn't know if this road trip was supposed to be our way of saying goodbye to one another and going out on a high note or our trying to remain friends. I told her that a part of me would always love the time we had spent together and how a little part of my heart would always belong to him for that reason, but no, I didn't think I loved him romantically anymore. I ended my story with saying that recent events helped me to see that.

"Good," she said when I was finally done with my story.

"Good?" *What part of that is good?*

"Yes. I'm glad you aren't with him like that anymore. I have it on good authority that someone on board thinks you're stellar." A wide grin broke out across her face.

Even without that smile, I knew she was talking about her brother. Already he made me feel things I hadn't felt for Dan in a long time. Butterflies flapped much faster in space.

"And by that smile, I take it you feel the same?"

"We'll see, Margot. I only just met you both, and you have to agree, the circumstances were highly unusual. I'm not going to rush it."

"I am rooting for the two of you. I agree with him, you're stellar." She giggled, then pushed off against the ground with her legs, sending her chair backward across the floor. "Now, how about we get to work?"

We spent the rest of the day business as usual, scanning headlines and watching news reports that mentioned anything questionable. I had come to enjoy this sort of work, and I liked helping Margot. I could see myself continuing this job if I remained on the ship. The variety of stories and reports always made the day go by quickly.

A half hour before our shift usually ended, Margot announced that we could leave early. She wanted to help me get ready to meet her parents. I was still nervous about meeting them, so I was grateful for the extra time to prepare myself. She had offered to let me borrow some of her clothes, so we were going to go to her room. I was curious to see how it differed from my converted cell.

We left the office and began walking down the hallway. However, we never made it to her room. The last thing I remember was someone smashing a cloth over my face. I saw stars, and everything went dark.

CHAPTER EIGHTEEN

JEREMIAH

I fumed all day after I was paged that morning and told I had to participate in another testing. I was livid when I found out that today's subject was a retake. He had come in the same night as Kyla, but with everything that had gone on, they put him back, erasing his memory of the few hours prior. Takings only took a half hour on average, but we always erased a few hours as a precaution. I couldn't believe that we'd have to do that again to this poor human. It couldn't have been good for one's psyche.

This male human had only the barest of files. I scanned both his retake file and his initial intake record on my retinal display while waiting for the crew to wheel him in. We didn't even know his name. This wasn't normal. Usually, takings were planned. And now, I would have to spend more time with him to do a thorough evaluation, discovering things that we would have learned through non-invasive observation had he even been considered for the taking prior to it happening. All signs pointed to his taking being sudden. I had a sinking feeling about this.

The intake crew wheeled the male into the room. Judging by his appearance, his age all but confirmed my suspicions. I couldn't let that stop me, however, I had a job to do no matter how much I didn't like it. I'd just have to come clean later and find out for sure. Why had I never bothered to ask Kyla what she was doing when she was taken?

Several hours later, I was dictating my notes, watching them appear on my retinal display, as I prepped the tray for testing. The evaluation had gone smoothly. I didn't expect anything less with this team. I had my preferred paralastysiologist—who spent the first five minutes of the exam apologizing profusely for what had happened with Jaxon—and the rest of the crew were all regulars who I could trust to do the job properly.

I was still fuming about what had happened to Kyla during her taking, but I had to admit it had kind of worked out for me. I was thrilled to have her in my life, but it didn't need to have happened that way. Although I hated that Jaxon was still on the Perihelion, I was happy he had been transferred to the farthest department from here. He was out of both of our lives, and I couldn't have been more grateful.

It wasn't meant to last.

"Jeremiah to Intake Room 2," a voice came through the in-room speakers. I knew that voice, and he was not supposed to be anywhere near the medical wing.

I slammed the tray table with my fist. "Comet! Someone call my dad. It's an emergency. Jaxon's in the next room. Send backup. Send this one back, too, and don't take him again," I yelled furiously as I ran out of the room, leaving my paralastysiologist and the rest of the intake team in stunned silence.

The door slid open to reveal Jaxon straddling Kyla on the gurney, pinning one of her arms down, while holding a syringe and scalpel as she frantically tried to kick at him. Two others, who I didn't recognize, held down her other arm and her legs. Margot lay tied up in the corner, eyes widening as she saw me.

"Stop right there, Jaxon." I charged the gurney and barreled into him, sending him sprawling off Kyla and onto the floor. Despite Kyla's now-free arm flailing around, his goons didn't flinch. *Idiots.* I pounced on Jaxon, wailing on him until the doors slid open once more.

"What is the meaning of all of this?" my dad yelled.

Everyone froze, including Kyla.

Panting, I rapidly tried to explain everything as backup arrived. I climbed off Jaxon, allowing my intake crew to haul him up and secure his hands behind his back. My paralastysiologist rushed in, followed by the Perihelion's security detail, and together they apprehended Jaxon's goons. It was then I noticed one of them was holding the syringe.

Aw, comet! I rushed over to Kyla's unmoving body. "Come on Kyla, wake up," I pleaded, repeatedly tapping her cheek.

"Butch, she's well under. It will be a while before she comes to ... if she does," my paralastysiologist said, putting his hand on my shoulder.

"Then I'm not leaving here until she does." I grabbed one of her hands, her warmth flooding through me and beginning to calm my racing heart. *Why did I refuse to hold her hand all week?* This is where I wanted to be—with her.

"Jeremiah," my dad began, "while she's under, you should test her."

I was horrified that my father could even suggest such a thing, and judging by the indignant squeal, Margot was, too. I shot a quick glance over my shoulder. "Can someone untie Go, please?"

My paralastysiologist made quick work of Go's bindings, and she flew over to the gurney, wrapping me in a hug. "She's going to be okay. She is, Jer."

"Jeremiah—" my dad began again.

"No," I bellowed. "I'm not going to make that decision for her, and how dare you even bring it up. This is Kyla, Dad. She's not some experiment."

"Jeremiah, enough's enough. I know you favor the girl or think she's stellar or whatever you kids call it these days, but we need to know if she's a prototype's descendant."

I didn't budge.

"Don't make me order you to do it."

Go scoffed audibly. "Daddy!"

I was so mad, I was shaking. *How can he ask me to do such a thing?* What a violation that would be against her. I could never do it.

Suddenly, it dawned on me as to why I hated my job so much. What I did was a violation to those who were taken. It was wrong, even if taking them was the only way we knew how to test them without giving our existence away. But I didn't have to test Kyla. I already knew.

"She is a prototype's descendant." I sighed, releasing her hand and bending down to kiss her, revealing her greening pale hand.

CHAPTER NINETEEN

KYLA

I don't know exactly how long I was out. By the way Jeremiah reacted when I woke up, one would have thought I had been asleep for days. I woke up with a start, nearly smacking Jeremiah in the face, but when I realized it was him, I gave him my biggest smile.

"Hi, Jer." My voice came out in little more than a whisper.

"Kyla, you're awake! You're going to be okay." Jeremiah smoothed the hair around my face, caressing my cheek, openly touching me—this couldn't have been good.

I didn't feel okay. I had a killer headache and once again couldn't feel my legs. I had a sneaking suspicion about what had happened.

As he helped me sit up, my legs dangling off the bed, he relayed the entire ordeal—Margot filled in the details prior to his arrival in the room. Hours had passed, and both of them had yet to leave my side. Jeremiah stayed next to me to keep me seated steadily.

"Margot, can you page Dad and have him come here, please?" Jeremiah asked.

"Sure. Be right back." She exited the room even though she easily could have called from the wall unit by the door. I had seen Jaxon use it before he pounced on top of me to help his minions hold me down. I silently thanked her for giving us some privacy.

After slowly lifting my leaden arm, I placed it on Jeremiah's shoulder. I attempted to pull him closer but couldn't make my forearm move how I wanted. I never wanted to be dosed with paralytic ever again.

But Jeremiah had read my mind, and he positioned himself between my legs. Pulling me close and bending over, he kissed my forehead and trailed kisses down the side of my face to my lips. The paralytic had dulled the icy sensation of his touch, but I could still feel his lips move across mine. I eagerly kissed him back.

The door to the room slid open, and someone gave a quick cough to let us know we had been caught.

Commander Taylor. Jeremiah had told me about what his father instructed him to do, and I was apprehensive about what would happen now that he was here.

"How are you doing, Kyla?" He actually sounded concerned, and was he blushing? His cheeks had taken on a slight brownish hue.

I went for polite honesty. "I've been better."

He cleared his throat. "I'd like to get right to the point, Kyla, but first I must apologize to you. I'm sure my children informed you of what I did."

I nodded. What was there to say?

"I'm sorry. It was wrong of me. I have been so focused on the mission that I failed to consider the individual—you. I hope you can forgive me. I hope you both can forgive me."

I nodded again and gave him a small smile. Out of the corner of my eye, I could see Jeremiah do the same. Commander Taylor didn't seem like the apologizing type, so I knew how hard it must have been to admit he was wrong.

"Kyla, you have had quite the week on board. Given this incident, I would understand if you were questioning your presence on the Perihelion."

He had that right. First, the circumstances of getting here, and now, being attacked. I was absolutely questioning my safety. I stood out. I was different. If Jaxon and his minions were any indication, not everyone was happy to have me on board. But did that matter? Did any of that matter? Everyone else had been so nice to me. Were they the only bad apples in the bunch? Was staying worth the risk?

I knew Commander Taylor was giving me the choice to go home. I could get off the spaceplane and go home to see my family. I could even try to work things out with Dan, figure out what this pause meant, but did I want to?

No. I didn't love him. Dan could never be my forever. If I went home, I would just be settling. And what would I be giving up? I looked at Jeremiah, his starlit eyes shining with a mix of caring concern and hopeful apprehension. I knew he wanted me to stay.

There was a chance that I wouldn't remember any of my time in space if they chose to dose me like a normal abductee when I left. It's exactly what would have happened to me had I been given the proper amount of paralytic when I was first taken. That's what happened to most people. They were left completely unaware or with fleeting memories believed to be nothing more than dreams. I refused to forget. I had to remain real. I needed to remember. I wanted to explore the universe and beyond. I was never satisfied with being stationary, and Jeremiah was already willing to let me soar.

Jeremiah squeezed my hand. How much had I craved this all week? Gazing into his celestial eyes, I smiled. This is what mattered. Him, me, us. Yes, it was worth the risk. I wanted Jeremiah.

But first, I needed answers.

Turning my head toward Commander Taylor, I asked, "What's going to happen to Jaxon?"

"We are holding him in a cell, and we will be returning to our home planet where he will be transferred to a more permanent facility."

"How long will that take ... to go back to your planet?"

"In hyperdrive, it will take a week to get there. Then I plan to give the spaceplane's residents a week's leave as I debrief with my superiors. It's been a long time since we've been home, and I'm sure we could all use a break, especially after this week."

"Will you come back here after that?"

"Yes, we will need to continue our mission. And it will take a week to return. We will be gone for three weeks. So what will it be, Kyla?" Commander Taylor asked in his deep, baritone voice, his amber galactic eyes giving me a weighty stare.

I didn't want to make this decision sitting down. I slid off the bed, Jeremiah spotting me in case my knees buckled like the last time I had been affected by the paralytic. I smiled at him standing next to me. I knew what he hoped for. The twinkling constellations of his eyes exposed his true feelings, and if my eyes had been like his, I'm sure they would have matched them, full of excitement and hope. I knew this was a once in a lifetime opportunity. If I chose to leave the ship, I knew I could be blowing my chance. But I had to go home first. It wouldn't feel right to just leave. It would hurt my parents, and Dan deserved some answers. I couldn't not say goodbye to them.

Standing shoulder to shoulder like good cadets in front of the commander, I slipped my hand into Jeremiah's and gave it a small squeeze. His hand tightened around mine, and I watched as the corners of his mouth tilted upward.

"Commander Taylor, sir, I would very much like go home"—I could feel Jeremiah tense next to me—"but only for the three weeks that you will be gone. I would like to return upon your arrival."

The tension left Jeremiah's body in a relieved sigh.

I don't think Commander Taylor was expecting that answer, and I watched his face as he considered it. "Very well, you have one hour to prepare for departure. Jeremiah, take her to the exit bay then prepare for lift off. I don't want to stick around. I'm sure we've given the Terraliens plenty to talk about with our being so low in the atmosphere this week."

"Yes, sir. Hundreds of sightings reported, sir," I replied, knowing Margot would enjoy my returning, as well. Now, she wouldn't be alone as she searched for Terralien reports of extraterrestrial sightings.

"Yes, well, let's get a move on, then. Carver, your new quarters have already been prepared and will be waiting for you to move in. And upon your return, you *will* submit to a formal testing to see if you are a prototype's descendant. I know what my son already suspects, but we need to know for sure. There will be no need for the paralytic if you agree. Dismissed."

I nodded at the commander. If it meant staying and helping Jeremiah and his people, I would let them conduct their test.

"Oh, and, Kyla?"

A broad grin across the commander's face met my inquisitive stare.

"Welcome aboard. I look forward to seeing you in three weeks. Let's reschedule that dinner for when you come back, shall we? I know my wife is dying to meet you."

I nodded, happy to see his tough exterior cracking slightly. "Yes, sir. Thank you, sir."

The commander strode out of the room, and Jeremiah and I slowly followed hand in hand. We had an hour to get to the exit bay, and I intended to use every minute of it.

An odd thought struck me. "Jeremiah, there are no potholes in space, right?"

He laughed, sending the butterflies that took residence in my stomach when he was around into a frenzy. "Potholes? Is that some sort of cooking instrument on Terral? No, we don't have those. But black holes and wormholes, yes. And you, my dear, will see them all when you come back." He pulled our joined hands to his mouth and gently kissed the back of my hand.

I liked the sound of that. I had never been so happy to have hit a pothole in my entire life. Together, we walked out of the intake room and into a brand-new journey.

ACKNOWLEDGMENTS

This book would not have been possible without the support of my husband Rob. Thank you for all of the dinner making, the chore doing, and the cat wrangling as I sat and wrote. This book would still be half-written and possibly abandoned if not for your belief in me. Thank you to my friends and family for their enthusiasm and support when I surprised them with the announcement that I had written a book. Thank you to Allie Barker, my original alpha reader, for falling for these characters and being my sounding board. Thank you to Desiree DeOrto for my beautiful book cover and for capturing Jeremiah and Kyla so well. Thank you to Melissa Ringstead of There for You Editing, for catching my typos and repeated words. Every author needs an editor, even one who is also an editor. To the authors at Wicked Ink Books, thank you for your anthology prompt that started me down the path with this story. Thank you to my UTOPiA family for all of your support, and especially to conference founder, Janet Wallace, for without the creation of this event, I would not be who I am today, and these words would never have been written. Mad love for you all. And finally, thanks to Twenty One Pilots for their song "Tear in My Heart," which served as inspiration for this story.

ABOUT THE AUTHOR

If you're still here, that means you've stayed to find out more about me, haven't you? Oh dear, what to say?

I've loved reading ever since I can remember and began writing stories in elementary school. The first story I ever wrote was about two bears who were best friends. One of the bears moves away and it makes the other one sad. But in the end, that bear moves back, and the story ends happily because the two bears can play together again. It was ten pages long. I was in kindergarten. It was called *Two Bears Playing.* Maybe I'll share it someday. I'm pretty sure my mom still has it.

My stories have evolved greatly since then. I like writing scifi, dystopian, and fantasy stories with a contemporary feel.

I like old things, cats, and ice cream. When not writing, you can usually find me editing as the Paisley Editor and enjoying life.

I live in Rhode Island with my husband Rob, who supports my bookish endeavors completely. He proposed to me on stage at UTOPiA2016 in front of an audience of authors and book industry professionals. It was perfect. We have two crazy cats named Jordy Purrson and Aaron Pawgers.

Come find me online:

Website: http://mariarosera.com
Facebook: http://www.facebook.com/AuthorMariaRosera
Twitter and Instagram: @PaisleyReader